BUI

UNIVE

Iain Leonard Rigby

Mobile Whale

© 2021 **Europe Books** | London
www.europebooks.co.uk – info@europebooks.co.uk

ISBN 979-12-201-0904-8
First edition: April 2021

Distribution for the United Kingdom: **Vine House Distribution ltd**

Printed for Italy by Rotomail Italia
Finito di stampare nel mese di aprile 2021
presso Rotomail Italia S.p.A. - Vignate (MI)

Mobile Whale

"Whales have become newly symbolic of real values in a world environment of which man is newly aware. Whales live in families, they play in the moonlight, they talk to one another, and they care for one another in distress. They are awesome and mysterious. In their cold, wet, and forbidding world they are complete and successful. They deserve to be saved, not as potential meatballs, but as a source of encouragement to mankind."

Victor Blanchard Scheffer

(American Biologist and the author of eleven natural history books)

Blackheart's father had told him long ago of an animal, not of the sea like them, but the land, a wolf. These animals hunted in packs and often caught prey much bigger than themselves.

The fishermen of old compared these wolves to Killer Whales, who they called Sea Wolves.

Blackheart would have liked to have been a wolf.

Chapter 1 – I Hear Reenging

Reuben was busy. Every day, more human rubbish appeared in the huge chamber. None of it could be eaten and would cause serious harm if not removed. Bottles, fishing nets, ropes, polystyrene, cans and plastic bags were unfortunately all normal. Occasionally, he came across an unusual item, which he kept hidden in his secret pile. Reuben disposed of the rest in abandoned sea caves and wasn't at all happy leaving it in the ocean.

"You know, keeping your insides free from rubbish William ees getting harder. All this plastic ees not good for your stomach, seemply orrible stuff. The oceans are not rubbish bins. Humans can be so selfish."

"There not all like that, Reuben. I was talking to a shoal of bottlenose dolphins the other day. Some are trying very hard, especially young people, but it takes time."

"Well, time ees something we do not have. My lobster brain might only be the size of a pea, but even I can figure this out."

"You're right, but we have to learn to get along, respect the land, oceans and skies. It's important, we try to help them understand the damage they are doing not only to marine life, but themselves and the planet."

"Then it ees about time they took their fingers out of their ears and started listening," huffed Reuben.

"RING–RING!"

"Monsieur, you never told me you had a phone. It ees reenging."

"Hilarious, Reuben. Blue Whales don't need phones. Have you been drinking too much Coral Cola again?"

"No! Maybe a little. Eet must be inside my head, but I do not theenk so."

"I wouldn't be so sure," chuckled William.

"Wait! The reenging has stopped. Perhaps I go crazy living inside your stomach for too long."

"Don't worry, my little lobster, you were always different, in a good way of course."

Reuben was French and had lost a claw after narrowly escaping being eaten by a giant octopus. The last thing he remembered was waking up inside William's stomach after drifting hundreds of miles. Luckily, Blue Whales only eat tiny Krill and soon after the unlikely duo decided to help each other. Reuben got rid of any rubbish the whale accidentally swallowed, and William kept the lobster safe from being eaten. Nurse sharks, octopuses, moray eels and triggerfish were only a few predators with a taste for lobster, with one claw or two.

"Ahh! You say the nicest things. I am happy you are my friend."

"You're welcome. We'll be surfacing soon. I think we could do with a bit of sea air. Clear the cobwebs."

"RING–RING!"

"Did you hear that?" asked William.

"No! I cannot hear any reenging from the reenging I am hearing because I am a crazy lobster. Can you hear reenging?"

"RING–RING!"

"Yes! Quickly, see if you can find where it's coming from."

It didn't take Reuben long. Underneath a pile of rubbish he had collected earlier that morning was a white — mobile phone.

"I've found eet! What should I do?"

"RING–RING!"

"Answer it," said William.

"What if eet's for you?"

"I don't think it will be for either of us. I must have swallowed it by accident close to the surface. I'm surprised it still works."

"RING–RING!"

"Pressing the button now… bonjour!"

"Hello. Oh! Thank goodness. Who's that?"

"It ees I, Reuben. To whom am I speaking?"

13

"I'm Clara. You've found my phone. Thank you, thank you, thank you."

"You are welcome, welcome, welcome."

"Where did you find it? I was sure I lost it when we visited Montevideo. I'm on holiday with my Mum on a cruise ship," explained Clara.

"Reuben," said William. "I'm swimming up. Make your way outside when I reach the surface."

"OK. We found eet after swimming up, I mean outside, in Montevideo."

"Is there someone else there?" asked Clara.

"My friend, William. We are also sailing on a boat... a big blue one."

"Cool! Could you post it to me please? I'm thirteen in three days, and it will be the best present ever. I'll pay for delivery and text you the port we're arriving next."

William broke the surface with a tremendous splash. The sea was calm, and the sun was shining as he opened his vast mouth, allowing Reuben outside.

"I'm not sure if that will be possible," said William, "we won't be on dry land for many months, perhaps years. We prefer the sea, sorry."

The phone went quiet, and Reuben could hear sniffling in the background.

"You big whale. I think she ees crying. Sometimes you can be so insensitive," Reuben scolded.

"I didn't mean…"

"Clara! Are you all right?" interrupted Reuben.

"I'm here," sniffed Clara.

"Why are you so upset? It ees just a phone. You can always get another one."

"You don't understand. It has all my pictures of Stephanie on it. My Mum kept telling me to save them to the cloud. Now it's all my fault."

"I don't mean to be nosey," said William, "but who is Stephanie?"

"She was my sister."

"You said, 'was!' What happened?" asked William.

"She became ill… and died last year. That's why the phone is so important to me."

"Oh, mademoiselle. We are so sorry and would be happy to return eet to you."

"You will?" said Clara.

"We would?" asked William.

"Wee," said Reuben. "Eet will be our great pleasure. Won't eet, William?"

15

"Um, yes, and we will bring it to you personally," mumbled William, feeling a little guilty, "make sure it doesn't get lost again."

"Please be telling your Mum you have spoken with us," insisted Reuben. "You cannot be meeting strange fish, I mean, strange people without a big human. Eet ees dangerous, OK!"

"Quite right," agreed William.

"I will and thank you. You are so kind. I can't wait to meet you."

"You will be in for a huge surprise," coughed Reuben.

"Gotta go, my Mum's coming. She doesn't know I've used her phone. I'll text you the details later, bye."

Chapter 2 – Locked Out

Whilst waiting for Clara's text, Reuben was enjoying the sea breeze and inspecting the phone. It was well protected in a plastic case, which must have prevented it from getting wet and breaking. Suddenly, the screen flashed.

"I theenk we have a little problem," said Reuben.

"Oh, I don't know. You're not that bad!" joked William.

"This ees no time for joking. The screen ees asking for something called the password."

"I see!"

"Do you know what this ees?"

"Yes. I mean, not exactly."

"That ees not helping," frowned Reuben.

"Humans use passwords to stop other people looking at their things."

"What theengs?"

"Anything!" said William.

"Sacré bleu! My brain ees hurting," Reuben moaned.

"Don't worry. It's usually four numbers. Very straight forward."

"Why didn't you say? Give me the numbers and I will put them in."

"I don't know the numbers, Reuben. They could be anything!"

"It ees lucky then I am the brains of this team. We will start with one, two, three, four then five, six, seven, eight and go from there."

"That would take forever, and it's unlikely the numbers would be so simple."

"Mon Dieu!" exclaimed Reuben. "With your super-sized head and mine, how hard can eet be?"

"Let me think for a minute," said William, closing his eyes.

Reuben wasn't the greatest thinker but thought he should at least try to help work out the answer...

Thirty minutes later.

"I've got it!" shouted William. "Reuben, are you asleep?"

"Huh! No, I was resting my eyes. All this theenking ees tiring work."

"Try these numbers, one, two, zero, seven. It's Clara's birthday. Remember, she said she was thirteen in three days' time."

"Ahh! Wee. Entering the secret, human code now..."

INCORRECT PASSWORD

"No, you are wrong, my blue friend."

"Are you sure you entered the numbers correctly?"

"Of course: one, two, zero, six."

"It's seven, barnacle brain, not six! Try it again."

"Stupid password... OK, eet's working, the screen ees opening. Now what?"

"Look for a small picture of an envelope near the bottom. On top should be a circle with the number one in it."

"How do you know so much about phones?" enquired Reuben.

"Because I'm nearly 70, I read a lot, and I'm smarter than you."

"That ees true, but you are not the most handsome. It is I, Reuben, who ees the prettiest lobster in the seas."

"You are, without doubt, one in a million crustaceans. Have you found it?"

"Wee. Opening our first human text."

hi ruby and willy

"Ahh, she called you Willy, and I am a Ruby. That ees so sweet."

"Get on with it," groaned William.

"Sorry… Willy."

tks for helping

"What ees t-k-s?"

"Thanks."

"You're welcome," said Reuben.

"No, tuna head, that's what it means - thanks."

arriving Rio Friday
ship called OCEAN STAR
have told mum

"I knew that. She has also told her mum."

"Sensible girl," said William.

b4n :) Clara x

"B, four, N! I theenk that might be her boyfriend."

"It's not a person, it's short for 'bye for now'".

"I see! Message ends with two dots and a curly theeng, Clara, kiss."

"You mean an emoji!"

"No, eet ees definitely not a monkey."

"E - M - O - J - I - not monkey," sighed William. "They're symbols and pictures' which describe how you feel. Clara's happy. Yours would be puzzled."

"Zut alors! I am surprised humans have lasted so long."

"Surprised you've lasted this long," muttered William.

"Begging your pardon, monsieur?"

"Nothing," coughed William, "let's get ready."

Chapter 3 – Risky Calculations

Reuben was excited and nervous, maybe more nervous, and a little scared. His last adventure had ended in disaster, and the thought of losing his one remaining claw made him feel shell sick. Still, it sounded a lot more fun than his normal day, but he was a little worried about William.

"I do not wish to be unkind," said Reuben, "but eet ees a long way in just three days. You are, as they say, not a young calf anymore. Perhaps I have been a bit hasty."

Reuben was right. It would be a hard swim even for a whale half his age, and dangerous. The quickest route would take them near Killer Whale hunting grounds, and Killer Whales were the only animal which could harm a Blue Whale. Even if Reuben and William slipped past undetected, whaling ships would seize any opportunity to hunt a Blue Whale if spotted, but the two friends had made a promise to Clara. William knew it was young people like Clara who were the planet's future, and he hoped she would remember their kindness one day.

"I have been doing some calculations," continued Reuben, who was surprisingly good with numbers.

Whilst William had been checking his flippers, tail and blowhole, the lobster had been working out how long the journey would take. Placing his claw behind his back, he paced up and down.

"It ees 1,045 sea miles from here to Rio. Even if you swim fast all the way, we will arrive in 3 days and 15 hours. This means we will be missing the boat."

William already knew he would have to navigate more dangerous waters and didn't want to alarm the lobster any more than was necessary.

"Then we'll have to take a shortcut to make up time."

"What type of shortcut?" asked Reuben.

"One I'd rather not make if we had a choice."

There was something in the whale's voice which worried Reuben, but the lobster knew he was right. They would never make it to the Ocean Star on time if they took the safest route.

"I am with you mon, Capitaine. We will do this for Clara, and all the silly humans."

William couldn't ask for a better friend. Reuben might only be small, but his heart was almost as big as his own, which was the size of an actual car. He'd never heard him complain once about his missing claw or seen him feel sorry for himself.

"Everything will be fine, plus, I have the best navigator in the oceans," William stated, flashing an enormous smile at the little lobster.

Reuben snapped smartly to attention, using his one claw to salute his captain.

"Then what are we waiting for," asked Reuben, as he marched back inside, holding his head high, "close the hatches, prepare to dive."

"Ahem!" coughed William. "Aren't you forgetting something?"

Reuben turned quickly and scuttled back to collect Clara's phone.

"Whoops!"

Chapter 4 – Sea Wolves

Blackheart had been leader of the group for ten seasons. Dozens of scars criss-crossed his body from challenges made by enemies he could no longer name. None had succeeded in defeating him; not even the Great White Shark was a match for his strength and cunning. Humans had given them the name Killer Whales. Blackheart liked that, except they weren't whales at all and belonged to the pathetic dolphin family.

Riptooth, Snagglefin and Whitetail were hungry. Snagglefin had gone ahead earlier to scout for food and was due back any minute. He was the weakest member of the clan, but the fastest, and his eyes moved constantly, even whilst resting.

Riptooth, meanwhile, circled impatiently. Bigger than Blackheart, he was slow yet powerful. His temper always got the better of him and he would often lose his meal because of his lack of patience.

Whitetail was new to the group, young and confident. Already a skilled hunter and well-liked by the others, he would soon challenge for leader, but not today. Blackheart would lead, and they would follow as Snagglefin returned.

"Humpbacks," grinned the whale.

Chapter 5 – Dark Skies

As the last rays of the sun faded across the waves above, Reuben had been double-checking everything was going to plan.

"We are making excellent progress," concluded Reuben, "at this speed we will arrive with time to spare."

"We!" grinned William.

"But of course, I am the Coach and you are the team captain."

"The weather has been kind, Coach, but I'm afraid rough seas are on the horizon."

William was right. In the distance, grey clouds rolled and jostled for position, eager to be at the centre of the gathering storm.

"Listen!" said Reuben. "Whale song."

William immediately recognised the sound vibrating through the water and surfaced to get a better view, as Reuben made his way outside. Heading towards them was a broad head covered in lumps, followed by another, smaller head.

"Humpback whales," said William. "A mother and her calf."

As they drew closer, it was customary to greet another whale.

"Blessings of wind and sea be upon you, sister," said William.

"And you, mighty brother. I am Suntide and this is my daughter, Moonsong."

"Welcome. I'm William and this is Reuben. Where is your pod?"

Suntide grimaced and Moonsong huddled protectively against her mother.

"We were attacked and became separated," explained Suntide.

"By who?" asked William.

"Blackheart!"

Reuben had always thought the Killer Whale was just a children's story told to frighten naughty fish and was both surprised and alarmed to learn he was real.

"Tell me everything," said William.

"There were three other Killer Whales. Quickgill and Coralsurf stayed and helped us escape, but they were no match for those monsters," sniffed Suntide. "It all happened so quickly, and they struck so fast. I don't know if any survived."

The skies darkened and rain began to fall as Reuben spoke with William quietly.

"What should we do?" asked Reuben. "This Blackheart ees a monster. We cannot leave them here on their own."

"He is a rogue creature, not like others of his kind and I've heard of his misdeeds. I will send them to a friend of mine, Waverider. His pod will take care of them. They will be safer with other humpbacks than with us, and we have a storm to navigate before the days end. Hopefully, it will help us remain unnoticed."

Chapter 6 – Black Storm

Like all of Blackheart's hunts, the ambush had been a success — of sorts. Snagglefin had discovered two male humpbacks, one female and her calf. They had easily caught up with the unsuspecting whales and struck like lightning from both sides, forcing each male to fight two Killer Whales.

Both whales fought bravely, allowing enough time for the mother and calf to escape. Blackheart had skilfully overpowered the first, injuring one of its large flippers. Riptooth and Snagglefin, however, had been careless and made hard work of the more experienced whale. The old humpback had delivered a powerful tail blow to Snagglefin's head, almost knocking him unconscious.

Riptooth had again lost his patience. Anger clouded his judgement, and he exposed his underbelly to the humpback's head, who slammed into him. Distracted by their stupidity, the younger, injured whale made good his escape. It was Whitetail who turned and dealt with the old whale. Younger and faster, he cruelly toyed with the humpback, cheered on by the others. Blackheart thought it unnecessary, but it didn't take Whitetail long to overpower the exhausted whale.

The Sea Wolves ate well that night, but Blackheart knew a leader was only as good as his last hunt. Perhaps it was time Whitetail accompany him tomorrow, after which they would hunt something bigger, much bigger.

•

With Suntide and Moonsong safely on their way, William headed towards the storm. Normally, he would swim under the strong current, but time was against them. Storms could also upset his sense of direction - another good reason to stay close to the surface. If they became lost, they would never reach Clara in time.

Above them the stormy seas rolled, and waves smashed together like knights charging into battle. The strong swell forced William to work twice as hard. Even Reuben, safe inside, could feel the whale being buffeted from every direction, as he struggled to stay on course.

"WILLIAM! ARE YOU OK?" shouted Reuben.

"We're nearing the heart of the storm," puffed William. "Hang on!"

Lightning flashed, illuminating the whale's huge shape underneath the waves. Thunder roared its delight and William felt as though a thousand hands were striking him, as his strong tail powered him forward. He was a Blue Whale and master of the oceans. Nothing would stop him.

Inside, Reuben's body shook, and he struggled to focus. The storm would have torn him apart, and he marvelled at the whale's strength and determination. He was trying hard not to panic and hadn't been this scared since his fight with the octopus. Shutting his eyes, Reuben thought of Clara and held on tightly.

A tremendous crack split the sky. William was exhausted and seconds away from diving when he felt the swell ease and the wind drop. The clouds lightened and the charging knights abandoned their fight, returning to the depths. They had made it through the storm.

"Reuben! Are you all right?"

"I am here. I think I have the queasy stomach."

"Come outside and get some fresh air whilst I rest for a short while. It's a cloudless night and you can check our course using the stars."

With William resting and Reuben gazing at the stars, both couldn't help wondering if the worst was behind them. Or had they just begun?

Chapter 7 – Ghost Ship

It had been easy to convince Whitetail to accompany him to the Galleon Graveyard. For the weak it was a place of fear, but to Blackheart it was home. To prove he was worthy to become leader, Whitetail would need to look upon the Golden Throne and return with an item of treasure.

Long ago, men in wooden ships with bright sails had fought a great battle. Only the spirits of the dead lived there now, trapped in a watery grave. Grey ships littered the seabed, broken and rotting. As Blackheart and Whitetail swam deeper, shadows appeared where no sunlight reached, and they could hear whispering. Every ship had holes where cannon fire had smashed hulls to pieces and toppled wooden masts. Rusting anchors, like headstones, marked the spot where each ship rested. Cannons waited patiently to be fired. Some still had their rowing boats attached to their hulls.

In the centre of the graveyard one ship towered above the rest. It had taken the most damage, but the mast remained unbroken. At the front of the wreck was a carving of a Killer Whale, and on the side of the ship was a name:

HMS Black Fish

Chapter 8 – Terrible Trawlers

Despite surviving the storm, William still had to make up time, which meant swimming into areas he would normally avoid. Reuben was mumbling to himself whilst checking their position.

"According to my calculations we are off the course," groaned Reuben. "These waters are not safe and look — ships."

Reuben was correct. Ahead, five fishing trawlers steamed towards them in a line. Each one was over half a mile away from the next. Whales often collided with ships and this was why William steered clear. The old whale, however, was more concerned with the nets they were using to fish.

Known as bottom trawlers, these large, weighted nets were the most destructive fishing method used by humans. Nothing could escape them, as they ripped along the seabed. It would take years for the delicate ecosystem to recover, as entire families would be forced to flee from their homes. If lucky, there would be a gap between the nets large enough for William to swim through, but it was risky. Any change in direction from the trawlers and he would have no time to avoid them.

"Why don't we go around?" suggested Reuben.

"Because it would take too long, and we don't have time," answered William.

"Then you leave me no choice. I am having to put my claw down. Returning the phone ees important, but so are you, my friend. I'm sure Clara would agree."

Like Clara, William knew what it was like to lose someone special, as he had lost his older brother when he was young. They had been playing hide the starfish when William became separated from his brother and a whaling ship spotted him. Unable to swim fast enough, the last thing William remembered was the sound of the harpoon whistling towards him. As it was about to strike, his brother had courageously leapt from the water and given his own life to save William.

That was over 60 years ago and although Blue Whales had long since become protected by laws, some humans still hunted them. He never forgot that terrible day and hated humans for many years. But hate is a destructive force, and nothing good ever comes from it. The Blue Whale had outlived many friends during his long life and learnt it was always better to forgive and show compassion than to hate others. Even Reuben, who'd lost his claw, never once wished any harm to the octopus who attacked him. Clara's generation had the power to change things for the better, and so did they.

"Don't worry. This is not the first time I've done this."

"Oh! How many times exactly?"

"Twice, including this one," said William. "Probably better if you go inside."

"We are about to become fish food," mumbled Reuben.

With Reuben safely inside, William dived back under the waves. He would have to guess where one net ended, and another began. There would be a space between each net to avoid them becoming tangled together, but he wouldn't be sure until he was much closer.

Even though William could no longer see the trawlers above, the noise created by the nets dragging along the seabed was deafening. It sounded like the ocean was being eaten, which it was. Crunching, ripping and cries of alarm grew gradually louder. William grimaced and felt awful for anything caught in the nets' terrible path. Fish swam past, fleeing for their lives, and only the fastest and strongest would survive. The rest would be caught in the nets, many of whom would be thrown lifeless back into the sea.

Clouds of sand like fog rolled towards William, making it difficult to see as he searched frantically for an opening. Glints of silver flashed like stars and shouts of help could be heard everywhere as the net crawled along the seabed, unstoppable in its hunger.

Something caught William's attention to his left. He couldn't see any sand clouds in an area not much wider than his body. That was the opening he'd been looking for, and luckily it wasn't far away. William would have to swim at an angle. There was no time to find a better position, and he would need to make a sharp turn at the last moment. If he got it wrong, they would join the hundreds of fish already trapped like fallen stars in a sea web.

"Reuben, hold tight!" shouted William. "We're going in."

Whilst Reuben tried not to think about what was happening, the whale increased his speed and was soon covered by the swirling cloud of sand. Swimming blindly, William had to time the turn perfectly and trust all his instincts. One second too soon or too late and they would become trapped in the net and drown.

Noise roared in William's ears, like waves crashing onto rocks, as he hit top speed. The net was now so close he could make out individual fish, terrified and helpless. Using his right flipper, he thrust it backwards with all his strength. The force generated swung his immense body immediately to the right, and he now faced the shimmering nets on both sides.

William had timed it perfectly and positioned himself in front of the opening. The nets passed by harmlessly and, within seconds, the water ahead was clear. William let out a sigh of relief. He was happy he'd made it through but saddened at the lives taken. The damage to the seabed was terrible and he couldn't bear to look at it for long. Gritting his teeth, the whale headed for deeper and safer waters. He was even more determined to prove that humans and sea animals could work together, and Clara was the key.

Chapter 9 – Reuben to the Rescue

After narrowly making it past the trawler nets, William hoped to avoid any more boats. He was also tired, and swimming was worryingly becoming a lot harder.

"Reuben, I think we have a problem. Something's caught on my tail and slowing me down. You'll have to go outside and look."

"Are we still in the deep water?" Reuben asked.

"Yes, but your hard shell should protect you," reassured William.

"You do not sound so sure! Are you sure you are sure? This ees making me unsure."

"I'm positive and don't want to surface until it's clear."

"Have you forgotten my eyesight ees not the best? Probably why I never saw the 'you know what' and look what happened."

Reuben was superstitious and never used the word octopus. He referred to them as 'you know what's' in case it brought him bad luck.

"I'm sorry, Reuben. Stay close and you'll be fine."

The lobster knew William wouldn't ask if there was any other way.

"What if I cannot free whatever ees tangling your tail?"

"I don't know," said William.

"William, you are a big fibber. Like Peekaboo with the long, wooden nose."

"You mean Pinocchio," corrected William.

"Wee. That ees what I said. Please, tell me."

William sighed. "If I don't get rid of the thing on my tail, I will get weaker, struggle to float and could drown."

Reuben hadn't realised the situation was so serious. The whale had always kept him safe and was determined to do whatever he could to help. He might only be small, with one claw, and afraid of the 'you know what's' but they had something special: friendship.

"Prepare to launch rescue lobster!" Reuben ordered. "But first I need to collect some theengs from my secret pile, which ees not a secret anymore because I have just told you my only secret, which was a secret!"

Reuben returned shortly with a ball of fishing wire and a yellow purse. On the front was a picture of a smiley face, and he was disappointed to learn it wasn't a monkey. He was also using a plastic cereal bowl for a helmet, just in case. Quickly tying the wire around his body, he attached the other end to one of William's baleen teeth.

"Rescue lobster, ready! Open scsame!"

The sea was black. Sunlight never reached this far down, and the secretive creatures who lived there liked it that way. Only those who learned to adapt in this strange part of the ocean could survive. Using his sense of touch, Reuben made his way to the top of William's head as the lobster moved forward. He tied the wire around barnacles, which had stuck to the whale's body. If Reuben lost his way, the wire would help guide him back to safety.

Rueben was over halfway when he imagined things creeping up on him: a giant squid, stingray, hammerhead shark. His legs felt like jelly, and he was about to turn back when he heard William singing their favourite karaoke song.

"Ohh, you make me live
Whatever the sea can give to me
It's you, you're all I see
Ohh, you make me smile now, Reuben
Ooh, you make me smile.

Oh, you're the best friend that I ever had
I've known you now such a long time
You're my seashine and I want you to know
That my feelings are true
I'm really proud of you
Oh, you're my best friend."

Encouraged by the whale's singing, Reuben took several deep breaths and continued. As he neared William's tail, the fishing wire suddenly tightened. Reuben tugged once, twice, then realised he'd run out of wire.

"Are you all right, Reuben?"

"I am fine. I theenk an old fishing net ees attached to your tail."

"It must have been dredged up from the seabed by those awful nets," said William.

"That ees what I am theenking. Please be maintaining radio contact while I investigate further."

"Be careful," said William, "over and out."

Reuben untied the wire and searched William's tail. His suspicions were correct. A fishing net with floats was attached, glowing faintly behind. The net was longer than a bus, but, luckily, had wrapped itself around in only one place. If he could find the right spot to cut, the net should break away. A sudden movement caught his attention and Reuben had the strangest feeling he was being watched.

"Stop being a baby lobster," muttered Reuben. "It ees your mind being tricky. William ees counting on you."

Returning to his task, Rueben soon found what he was feeling for. Opening the purse, he removed a small pair of scissors and began cutting. With only one claw it was fiddly, but gradually the net loosened.

"William, this ees rescue lobster. Eet ees working, over."

"Well done," said William. "I knew you could do it."

"I am nearly…"

"Say again, Reuben! Nearly what?"

But there was no response.

In an instant, William knew something was horribly wrong. Worse, though, he didn't know what to do.

Chapter 10 – Sucker Punched

Whilst Reuben had been busy, something in the darkness had taken a keen interest in the lobster. Using the net as cover, it crept silently until it was within striking distance. Reuben saw the long arm at the last moment and ducked. Another arm smacked into his side, causing him to drop the scissors. A third appeared from the gloom, as Reuben frantically dodged several deadly tentacles.

"AGGHHH! YOU KNOW WHAT," shrieked Reuben, "HELPPPPP!"

Already on red alert, William reacted immediately.

"REUBEN! GET UNDERNEATH THE NET, NOW."

Reuben rolled forward, dodging tentacles, and squeezed under the net. Backing away from the slithering arms, lights pulsed from its body. Jaws snapped down bouncing off his helmet and was grateful for the cereal bowl. Octopus where clever animals though, and patient. From several direction's tentacles crawled under the net, searching. Reuben was trapped.

But something Reuben had said earlier about being a Coach gave him hope. A good Coach never gave up and would always fight to the end. Realising the octopus was using an arm to prevent itself floating away,

Reuben had an idea. If it worked, it would get rid of the octopus and the net, but he wouldn't get a second chance.

Many years ago, Reuben had learnt a secret language from his Grandfather who once lived on a ship, HMS Sirius, during his adventures in the Royal Navy. It was called 'Morse Code' and Reuben had taught William how to send and understand these clever signals without talking. By making short and long clicks, they could spell out words and send messages.

William was convinced the lobster had been eaten when Reuben's clicks echoed through the water. The whale had no time to celebrate and paused only long enough to receive the message:

"EMERGENCY SURFACE"

With a powerful flick of his tail, William raced towards the surface. The sudden change in direction surprised the octopus. Losing its grip, it was sucked backwards past William's tail. Reuben cheered, but the octopus wasn't beaten yet. Using its arms like grappling hooks, it caught the net.

No longer attempting to hide, the angry octopus scrambled back towards the lobster. It was now or never. Emerging from the net, Reuben crawled towards the place he'd cut. Realising what was about to happen, the octopus launched itself in a desperate attempt to reach the lobster. Reuben inserted his claw, closed his eyes, and pressed down with all his strength.

"SO LONG, SUCKER!" shouted Reuben.

The net snapped and whipped backwards, hitting the octopus in the face. The net sunk quickly, covering the octopus completely and taking its new prisoner down into the murky depths below. Reuben could hardly believe it. He'd beaten the octopus! Not only that, the net was free.

"Are you all right?" gasped William, reaching the surface.

"We did eet!" shouted Reuben. "The octopus and net are both gone!"

"That was incredible!" cheered William. "Wait, you said the word, octopus."

"And I defeated the monster like Sea Superman, but I do not wear red underpants. I am already red — you would not see them."

"There's no sign of the trawlers," laughed William. "We are back on course, my friend."

Super Reuben quickly collected the fishing wire and made his way inside. With Reuben safe and William swimming freely again, it was time to continue their journey.

Chapter 11 – Golden Crown

Whitetail was eager to complete the test and almost laughed when Blackheart explained what he had to do. Ghosts didn't frighten him, and things would change under his leadership, starting with Blackheart. The old whale who watched from a hole above, had become weak. It was time for him to step aside. All Whitetail had to do was to return with an item of treasure. It was so easy.

As Whitetail made his way down into the depths of the shipwreck, an eerie glow escaped from cracks in the rotting floorboards. The water felt strangely colder and thicker, like mud, as voices began to whisper.

"Down, down, down below
amongst the dead king you must go.
To look upon the crown of old,
and prove you are a whale so bold.

Touch not the crown upon his head,
or seal your doom and you'll be dead!
And like the King, you will lie
upon the treasure piled so high."

Whitetail felt uneasy. There was nothing alive in here which could harm the Killer Whale, but something felt wrong as he wriggled through another hole. Brushing aside a heavy curtain of seaweed, he found what he was searching for.

A skeleton, washed clean by the sea, sat grinning on a throne. On its head was a silver crown, and all around was a mound of treasure. It was worth a fortune to humans, but to Whitetail it held no value. It only proved he'd mastered his fear and looked into the eyes of the dead king. But what to take? A sword, precious jewels, gold bars, diamonds, coins? It needed to be something special. Whitetail grinned. It was time for the king to give up his crown.

•

Blackheart watched as Whitetail decided which item of treasure to choose. Whilst the whale had been busy with his task, Blackheart had also been preparing and he was also ready.

•

Taking the crown in his strong mouth, Whitetail chose not to heed the warning, which once more whispered in his ears.

"Touch not the crown upon his head,
or seal your doom and you 'll be dead!"

As soon as the crown was lifted, the dead king's skeleton broke apart, as if the crown were the only thing which had been holding it together for centuries. Whitetail couldn't help but chuckle. He would now become leader of the Black Fish.

As soon as Blackheart heard the skeleton breaking, he pushed the huge cannon. It smashed through the wooden deck into the throne room, roaring its arrival. Clouds of sand and bubbles flew upwards, causing Blackheart to back away, as a terrible cry pierced the water.

Everywhere was silent as Blackheart peered through the hole. Slowly, the water cleared to reveal the cannon lying on its side. It had completely crushed the king and his throne. Treasure had spilled everywhere, mixing with broken timbers. Underneath the throne and treasure was a tail, a white one. Pity thought Blackheart; he would have made a good leader if he wasn't such a fool. Blackheart turned to leave, his black heart laughing.

On his return, Snagglefin and Riptooth suspected some foul deed had taken place but were too afraid to question Blackheart. It was not unusual for males to fight, and Blackheart had never lost a challenge. Whitetail had been beaten and, like always, they would follow the strongest leader. It was now the perfect opportunity for Blackheart to prove he was still in charge.

"Gentleman, I think it's time we cast our net wider," announced Blackheart.

"But we don't use nets," Riptooth replied, a little confused — which didn't take much.

"The boss means we need to think bigger," explained Snagglefin.

"Quite so," continued Blackheart, "and what is the biggest thing in the seas?"

"Icebergs," said Riptooth.

"Oh, yeah," agreed Snagglefin. "Did you know you can only see 10% of an iceberg on the surface? The rest of it is underwater."

"And the largest iceberg ever seen was 208 miles long and 60 miles wide," added Riptooth, "bigger than the country Belgium."

Blackheart slapped both whales sharply on the nose.

"Thank you for that most interesting Geography lesson in floating blocks of ice," growled Blackheart. "I was thinking of something we can sink our teeth into."

Riptooth would eat anything and had difficulty choosing. Snagglefin rubbed his nose, then it dawned on him.

"A whale!"

"Snagglefin, you are cleverer than you look," grinned Blackheart. "But not just any whale, the largest of whales, the mighty Blue. And I have received information where one is heading, right now. Come on lads. Follow me."

Chapter 12 – Hunted Angels

After his escape from the octopus, Reuben had taken a well-deserved nap, whilst William continued towards Rio. Feeling refreshed, he woke to discover a new message on Clara's phone.

"William! We have another texty message."

Hi how r u
is everything ok
will u arrive on time today
Clara x
mum thinks u r guardian angels

"Did you hear that? We are sea angels, but instead of wings you have flippers and I have a claw."

"Some other good news, we will arrive a few hours before they set sail," said William. "Have you been thinking how you're going to deliver the phone to Clara?"

"I am, how you say, working on eet," said Reuben. "Maybe we can disguise ourselves and slip into the harbour unnoticed."

"Please tell me you're joking!"

"No! You can be a yellow submarine and I will be the fearless Captain. We will have to find some waterproof paint first. I also have a hat and bineoccles somewhere."

"Sometimes, Reuben, I wonder what's wrong with you, and submarines aren't yellow."

"Au contraire mon ami, eet ees in the song by the Beatle men."

"It's, 'The Beatles', and they're called, binoculars."

"That ees what I said. I suppose we can do what we always do."

"Make it up as we go," said William.

"Exactement," grinned Reuben. "Next stop, Rio."

•

The crew of the Hoeruhanta had performed their duties well during the voyage. The ship's name meant - Whalehunter, and they had caught many whales during their three months at sea. One more and the crew would receive a handsome bonus on their return.

Catching whales was carried out to help scientific research, or so many believed, and there was always room for another in the large hold. Reports of three Sea Wolves in the area had so far been the only whale activity. Killer Whales were of little value though, and the crew were prepared to wait. A profitable venture required the biggest prize, and none could escape the Hoeruhanta.

•

The Black Fish had travelled all night and arrived well before William was expected. Blackheart had discovered the information after finding an octopus trapped in an old fishing net. The pathetic creature had been happy to share which direction the whale was headed. In return, Blackheart had promised to free him. Unfortunately, he'd made no such promises about not eating the octopus afterwards. Blackheart chuckled. Such was life in the oceans: eat or be eaten.

The arrival of the Hoeruhanta, however, was not part of Blackheart's plan. Whilst it was unlikely, they would be attacked, Riptooth and Snagglefin were nervous. If the ship spotted the Blue Whale first, it would be impossible to match its speed and power. Blackheart's plan would then be in tatters, and he would look like a fool. Worse, a challenge to his leadership was possible, perhaps this time from both idiots.

No, it was vital they caught the whale by surprise and finish the job quickly. Snagglefin would attack the whale's tail using his speed and agility, causing the whale to panic. Riptooth would then join the attack and use his powerful body to cause the whale to surface. With the whale fighting on two sides, Blackheart would strike from underneath. It was a dangerous strategy, as he could easily collide with Riptooth and Snagglefin and cause serious injury to himself or them. It was worth the risk, however, and if one got injured, so be it. Sea Wolves did not shed tears.

Chapter 13 – Are We There Yet?

Snagglefin had been waiting patiently for William's arrival. The Blue Whale was unaware he was being followed, and Snagglefin kept a safe distance. He'd seen Blue Whales before, but this was by far the largest and not an animal to be taken lightly. One blow could seriously injure any of the Killer Whales.

Surprise, speed, and numbers would be used to their advantage. Slower and less agile, the Blue Whale would become gradually weaker. Unable to defend itself, all three would then strike as one. But as Snagglefin hurried back with his report, a nagging doubt surfaced. There was something different about this whale that he couldn't quite put his fin on.

•

"Are we there yet?" asked Reuben.

"Yes," said William.

"Really?"

"No!"

"Then why did you say that?" tutted Reuben.

"Because you've been asking me the same question every ten minutes. And, before you ask, about 35 nautical miles."

"That ees spooky. You are like a mind reader. What am I theenking now?"

"I don't know."

"You don't, but your mind does. Concentrate, eet will speak to you."

William knew the chances of Reuben giving up asking were slim, but he had a few tricks up his flipper. What Reuben didn't know was the lobster often talked in his sleep.

"You're hoping someone will build a marble statue of you fighting an octopus whilst holding a mobile phone to the sky," declared William.

Reuben couldn't believe it! That was exactly what he'd been thinking. That meant William would know he'd eaten the last pack of jellyfish beans earlier. And, if he didn't, he did now, as Reuben had just thought it.

"Let's see what's happening up top," grinned William. "We should be able to see the coast by now."

Reuben was still trying to figure out how William had read his mind as he stepped outside. Sunshine bathed the sea, and the skies were clear. Visibility was excellent and they could see the coast of Brazil in the distance.

Close by, Gannets were hunting small fish and squid. Reuben admired how they would plummet towards the surface. Folding their wings back tightly at the last second, they sliced through the water with ease and speared the unfortunate fish beneath.

As he watched the birds' daredevil acrobatics, Reuben noticed a small, black shape not far behind. He tried shielding his eyes from the sun's glare to get a better look, but whatever it was had disappeared.

"Hmm! Strange," said Reuben.

"What is?" asked William, who had been enjoying a few minutes silence.

"I thought I saw something. A black shape, maybe white. Eet ees gone. My eyes are not used to the sunlight."

"I'll get you a pair of sunglasses when we arrive in Rio," suggested William. "C'mon, let's get going."

Chapter 14 – Flight or Fight

As they neared Rio, and the end of their journey, something Reuben had said earlier was troubling the Blue Whale. Waters this close to land would normally be a hive of activity, yet they were unusually quiet for the time of year. All whales were born with good instincts, which they used to survive, and William's alarm bells were ringing. His brother had taught him the importance of listening to the ocean and ignoring her at your peril.

In comparison, lobsters had almost no survival instincts and, like Reuben, found themselves in danger all too often. William could hear the lobster whistling whilst "sprucing himself up" to meet Clara and her Mum. Perhaps he was just tired. It had been a tough three days and once they delivered the phone a holiday was definitely in order: Bermuda maybe, or even Cuba.

William didn't even realise at first that something had hit him as his tail swung to the right. His first thought was he'd collided with a ship which was impossible as he wasn't close to the surface, so perhaps it was a submersible craft.

Seconds later, another blow smacked into William's tail. Shocked, he caught a flash of black and white swimming swiftly away. That was it! The thing Reuben thought he'd imagined earlier was a Killer Whale! William's instincts had proved correct. He was being hunted.

"William! Are you OK? Did we hit something?"

"Killer Whale!" shouted William. "It's been tracking us!"

"Mon Dieu! What are we going to do?"

"Black Fish don't hunt alone. I'm heading for the surface."

William quickly breached the surface, but there was no sign of the Killer Whale. Judging from its weak blows, it was small but fast. Filling his lungs with air, William dived back under the ocean.

"Has it gone?" whispered Reuben.

William couldn't possibly see in every direction. His tremendous size was now a disadvantage. Seconds later, a second Killer Whale appeared, and William could do nothing except brace for impact.

Much bigger than the first, this killer rammed William headfirst, causing Reuben to fly from one side of the whale's stomach to the other. If not for William's enormous rib cage all the air would have been knocked out of his lungs. Almost immediately, the smaller predator battered William's tail again. With William fighting on both sides Blackheart watched from below, eager to join the attack. His plan was working perfectly.

William had to even the odds and had no idea if more whales were out there, ready to strike. Snagglefin, meanwhile, brimmed with confidence. He was far too quick for the Blue Whale and noticed his large tail wasn't moving. Distracted by thoughts of becoming leader,

Snagglefin underestimated the whale and came too close. The Killer Whale knew he'd been tricked. With a snap of his tail, William landed a mighty blow against Snagglefin's head. With no time to get clear, it smashed into his face.

Blackheart watched as Snagglefin was sent spinning into the depths below, a long stream of bubbles shooting from his mouth. His fight was over, perhaps for good. The Blue Whale was clever, and patience was necessary.

Riptooth saw Snagglefin sink quickly. Angry, he prepared for another strike as the whale headed once again for the surface. Blackheart felt the blow pulsate through the water as he moved into position underneath. Such was the force created by Riptooth, William spun around and now faced the opposite direction to which he'd been swimming in.

William grimaced. He couldn't take many more blows like that. Before he could steady himself, he saw a third whale hurtling towards him from below like a torpedo. With his underbelly exposed, Blackheart delivered a perfect strike before darting quickly away.

William floated to the surface, dazed and badly shaken. He shook his large head. Flight was now his only option, but the coast was too far, and things looked hopeless. Nearby, black fins cut through the water, circling.

"Reuben?" coughed William.

"I am here. Are you hurt?"

"I'm fine," lied William. "Listen carefully. It's Blackheart. You have to leave."

"You mean, abandon whale!"

"Yes!"

Reuben didn't even hesitate in his response.

"Never!"

"Please, Reuben. There's no time."

"Listen to me, you big whale. We have a little girl waiting and I will not be letting some stupid black whales stop us. You are a Blue Whale. Master of the Oceans. And my best friend. I would never leave you alone with these creatures."

A lump formed in William's throat. No matter what he said, he knew Reuben would not leave. Gritting his 350 baleen teeth, a fierce determination blazed through the old whale. Inspired by the words of his friend and Coach, he would not turn tail and run. They were a team. And they would fight!

Chapter 15 – Blackheart

The crew of the whaling ship kept their distance and watched the Sea Wolves circling the exhausted whale. It would now be even easier to catch the Blue Whale, as they had done an excellent job bringing it to the surface. With the harpoon crew in place and already discussing how they planned to spend their bonus, it was time to finish the job.

•

"Reuben! Do you trust me?"

"Wee! Of course."

"I need you to be my extra set of eyes on the surface. Can you do that?"

"But you won't last long up there."

"Let me worry about that. Ready?"

"Ready as a lobster about to make his escape from a hot pan of onion soup."

"GO!" shouted William.

As soon as William opened his mouth, Reuben sprinted outside as the two Killer Whales edged closer. The lobster felt like the starter on a menu and William was the main course. With no idea what William was planning, Reuben tried to keep an eye on both whales. Even Mantis Shrimps with the most advanced eyesight of any animal would have struggled.

"HANG ON!" roared William.

Driving his tail down, William shot forward. Riptooth and Blackheart were slow to react, already thinking the hunt was over. The fool couldn't possibly outrun them on the surface and had panicked, thought Blackheart. It would be his first and last mistake as he set off in pursuit.

At exactly the same time, the Hoeruhanta increased knots and steered straight towards the Blue Whale and its pursuers.

"Reuben! How far are they?" gasped William.

"Close, very close, and getting closer. I think eet ees Blackheart. The fat one cannot keep up."

Reuben looked around desperately for other escape routes. Only then did he see the whaling ship.

"William, there's a…"

"I know," interrupted William.

William had again read his mind, as Reuben looked away in shock.

"Concentrate on Blackheart," instructed William. "Let me know when he is about one length of me away!"

"OK," trembled Reuben. "William… I'm scared."

"It's OK, Reuben. So am I. Remember, keep your eye on Blackheart."

Blackheart was impressed at the Blue Whale's strength. The whale was nearly at full speed, but Killer Whales were faster, and Blackheart was gaining every second. Riptooth had shouted some kind of warning, but Blackheart ignored the fool. He would finish the Blue Whale on his own. He didn't need anyone else's help. All the animals of the ocean would then tremble before their new master.

•

William had noticed the whaling ship seconds after reaching the surface. Never in his long life had he faced such a difficult choice. With the ship gathering speed, he could do only one thing: swim towards the Hoeruhanta.

Chapter 16 – ホエルハンタ - Whalehunter

The explosive harpoon was loaded carefully into the large gun. Attached to the harpoon were strong cables with hooks designed to penetrate a whale's thick skin. Once lodged in its body, there was no escape, and the helpless whale would be reeled onto the ship.

•

William thought of his brother as the Hoeruhanta loomed closer. Sunshine reflected menacingly off the cold, steel gun. Reuben watched Blackheart, terrified, as the Blue Whale's heart pumped faster than ever before, delivering oxygen to starving muscles.

Faces of crew members, cruel and unforgiving, could now be seen manning the harpoon. William closed his eyes and remembered the games he used to play with his brother. A great calmness descended on him, as he listened to the ocean and waited.

•

Blackheart felt unstoppable. He laughed when he saw a lobster sitting on top of the whale, watching him closely. Nothing else mattered: The sun, the sky — not even the ocean, as the Blue Whale was getting slower every second. Blackheart hit maximum speed and prepared to deliver his killer blow.

73

"NOW!" shouted Reuben.

"FIRE!" shouted the gunner.

William slammed his tail and left flipper down with every ounce of strength left in his body. Blackheart was shocked. He'd never seen a whale turn so quickly, displaying such mastery of the sea.

Had Blackheart listened to the ocean and Riptooth's warning, he would have seen the danger. But it was too late. The harpoon sunk deep into the killer's side. It had missed the fleeing whale by a fraction, and only then the whale narrowly avoided colliding with the prow of the whaling ship.

Rueben opened his eyes to see Blackheart floating sideways, lifeless on the surface. Riptooth had already fled at the sight of the Hoeruhanta and would learn later of his leader's fate. Angry curses came from the deck of the ship. The crew had missed and would not receive any bonus on this trip. It would also take hours to dislodge the dead whale and retrieve the harpoon, by which time the Blue Whale would be far away.

William slowed down. Had there been any other way, he would have chosen not to lure Blackheart towards the Hoeruhanta? But the Killer Whale had made his choice and William had bravely protected his friend and kept his promise to Clara.

"Reuben! Are you all right?"

"Wee. No. I hope we never, ever, have to do that again," sniffed Reuben. "We soooo need a holiday."

"Yes, we do," agreed William, "and, Reuben… thanks."

"What for?" asked Reuben.

"For being my friend."

"Stop it, you silly whale. We still have a phone to deliver. And no, I am not crying, eet ees the wind. Do you have a tissue?"

Chapter 17 – Rio

Their short journey to Rio held no more surprises. William was a little sore but would heal quickly and Reuben had never been this excited since he'd first discovered bubble wrap.

Gasps of amazement and cries of alarm quickly spread along the harbour entrance, as people gathered to see if William and Reuben were real or a practical joke.

"I'm thinking the yellow submarine wasn't such a silly idea," whispered William.

"Why are they staring?" asked Reuben. "You theenk they had never seen a lobster before."

"Just try to look casual. Smile. Give them a wave or something," advised William.

William and Reuben noticed lots of people were taking pictures on their phones as they waved. Children waved back and everybody was pleased to see these ocean wonders, at least almost everyone.

In the distance, two speedboats with flashing red lights had been alerted and made their way swiftly over to the whale and the lobster.

"Do you theenk they are here to escort us?" Reuben asked.

"More likely here to arrest us," said William worriedly.

"What! This ees a free ocean and we have fish rights. They will not lock me up in a fish tank. Rapido! We need to make a swim for it."

"What about Clara?" reminded William. "And I can't turn around "Rapido" without hurting someone."

"You're right," agreed Reuben. "We have to reach the Ocean Star and eet ees lucky I have a plan."

"I was afraid you'd say that." William moaned.

"Using my acting skills, I will clutch my chest, faint and fall into the water. Whilst everyone ees watching me drown, you slip past quietly."

"Brilliant!" said William.

"Really! I wasn't so sure."

"I'm joking. For starters, you're a lobster and can breathe underwater…"

"That ees true."

"Then, why is somebody going to rescue a lobster who is perfectly at home in the sea?" questioned William.

"Ahh! You have a point."

Whilst discussing Reuben's plan, the two friends had forgotten about the speedboats sent to investigate. At the front of the nearest boat was a large man wearing chrome sunglasses and holding a microphone.

ATTENTION — BIG WHALE & LITTLE CRAB
THIS IS THE MARINHA DO BRASIL
YOU ARE SWIMMING IN A RESTRICTED AREA
LEAVE IMMEDIATELY!

"It's the Brazilian Navy," whispered William. "Don't say anything stupid."

"Do not worry. You forget, I am French, and crabs have excellent manners. Bonjour le crétin. First, I am a lobster, perhaps you are needing better glasses."

"Wonderful," sighed William.

Chuckles came from the crowd and some nodded their agreement.

"My name ees Reuben, and this ees William. In case you were wondering, he ees a whale, a blue one."

Cheers and laughter could be heard from all around as Reuben played and bowed to the crowd. William had heard enough and thought it better if he negotiated entrance passes to the harbour.

"Apologies! My friend has recently been attacked by an octopus and received several blows to the head. He's also from France," William explained.

The sailor nodded, as though that at least explained his odd behaviour.

"We're here to deliver a mobile phone to a young lady, Clara. Perhaps you know her. No? She's a passenger on the Ocean Star. It's not our phone because we don't use them. I don't have fingers and Reuben only has one claw. I swallowed it by accident…"

"William," muttered Reuben, "you're waffling. Perhaps we should just show them the phone."

"Good idea," agreed William.

Reuben held up the phone as more people arrived to see what was going on. The sailors talked amongst themselves before microphone man spoke again.

ENTRY IS DENIED
RETURN TO THE SEA IMMEDIATELY
FORCE WILL BE USED IF NECESSARY

Some people in the crowd booed; everyone thought they should be allowed to explain further. With lots of visitors using their mobiles to record what was happening, the officer in charge was becoming nervous. The last thing he needed was an international incident with a Blue Whale and a French lobster. Plus, Brazilian people were known all over the world for their friendliness, which he supposed included sea animals, too.

PLEASE EXPLAIN WHY THE
PHONE IS SO IMPORTANT?

The crowd cheered and shouts of "Bravo senhor" could be heard. Pleased at their reaction, the officer saluted and puffed out his chest, signalling for quiet. The crowd all waited expectantly.

"I think that's our turn," said William, "over to you."

"What should I say?"

"I don't know," said William, "just speak from the heart."

"Ahem. Bonjour! We come in peace, unless you are an octopus! Ha, ha, my little lobster joke. On this phone are many beautiful pictures of Clara's sister, who I am sad to say ees now in heaven. Clara forgot to save the photos to the cloud theeng in the sky.

If we do not return eet, her memories will fade, and Clara's heart will become sadder every day until eet can no longer be mended. We are here to make sure that does not happen, as there ees too much heartache in this world already... We also like football."

Everywhere was silent, and Reuben thought he'd ruined their chances. Then, a single clap could be heard, as Reuben turned around to see microphone man with a tear in his eye. The rest of the sailors joined in, followed by everyone in the crowd, who were cheering, clapping and hugging each other. William couldn't be prouder of his fabulous friend.

"They must really like their football," grinned Reuben.

Chapter 18 – Captain's Invitation

Clara and her Mum were at the stern of the ship looking out over the harbour. They had spent the morning relaxing on the famous Copacabana Beach, watching beach vendors selling everything from fans to kites. Favela kids had showed off their football skills and lots of people played volleyball and beach tennis. Her Mum had tried a Caipirinhas, the most popular cocktail in Brazil, and purchased a yellow and red sarong with a sunset theme for Clara. Returning on board after lunch, they were waiting patiently for William and Reuben.

Clara noticed a man in a white uniform, with gold epaulettes speaking to Inacio, their favourite waiter. Pointing in their direction, the large man headed towards them.

"Captain Jasper," winked Clara's Mum, "fancy meeting you here."

"Mrs Anderson. And this must be Clara. How do you both like Rio?"

"Please, call me Amanda. It's fabulous, thank you."

"Amanda it is. Now, I have it on good authority that today is a special day. Clara, on behalf of the crew of the Ocean Star, may I wish you a happy 13th birthday!"

"How did you know it was my birthday? Mum…"

"And to celebrate this auspicious day, it would be my honour if you would both dine with me at Captain's table this evening."

"Thanks," gasped Clara, blushing, and wondered if this is what it felt like to be famous.

"We'd be delighted," said Amanda, who was already thinking about which dress to wear.

"Excellent. Then I will ask my second in command to collect you from your cabin and escort you to the Mistral Bar for cocktails. And don't worry, Clara, I like cheeseburgers and fries, but please don't tell my steward, Reginald. He's trying to put me on a diet. Now, if you ladies will excuse me, I have a Superhero fancy dress competition to judge. I will see you tonight."

"OMG! Mum, that was so embarrassing," squirmed Clara.

"Surprise! Well, it's not every day you're thirteen. Should be fun. Can you hear that? Sounds like someone's already in the party atmosphere."

Only a few minutes ago, Amanda and Clara had seen two naval boats speeding past and wondered if they had been sent to investigate the source of the noise.

"I hope William and Reuben get here soon," said Amanda, "I need to wash all this sand out of my hair."

"They will," said Clara, crossing her fingers.

Chapter 19 – We're Here

With the Brazilian Navy escorting them, William and Reuben arrived safely at the rear of the Ocean Star. News had spread throughout the ship and quite a few passengers had come down to see the strange visitors.

"Inacio! What's all the fuss about?" asked Amanda.

Inacio placed his drinks tray on the table and sat down.

"Apparently, senhora, a Blue Whale is looking for a passenger on our ship. If this is true, then I am Tom Cruise, but taller and better looking. Personally, I think people have been drinking too many Caipirinhas. They say there is also a lobster with a white mobile phone. Maluco! How you say, crazy people."

As Inacio continued collecting glasses, Clara looked at her Mum.

"You don't think...?" asked Clara.

"Only one way to find out," said her Mum, passing her phone to Clara.

Clara dialled her own mobile number, as they made their way towards the lowest part of the ship.

•

Reuben, meanwhile, had for the moment forgotten about Clara's phone. He was enjoying all the attention and posing for people taking photographs. Suddenly Clara's mobile rang, making the lobster jump and reminding him why they were here in Rio.

"Ello... Clara, ees that you?" Reuben asked tentatively.

"Reuben! Hi. Yes, it's me, Clara. Um, are you both at the back of the ship?"

"Wee. We are like poppy stars and are having a whale of a time. My little joke! Are you nearby? We are looking forward to meeting with you."

By now Clara and her mum had joined the small group of passengers on the bottom deck, marvelling at the incredible sight.

"Over here," shouted Clara waving. "I'm wearing a red and yellow sarong."

"There," smiled William, turning his huge head, "and that must be her mum."

"How are we going to deliver the phone safely?" whispered Reuben, waving frantically.

"I might know someone who can help," said William.

Following Reuben's instructions, Clara and her mum made their way off the ship and walked towards a small jetty. Waiting to collect them was the Brazilian officer who helped them into his speedboat. Meanwhile, William had swum into the middle of the harbour where there were fewer cameras to distract Reuben.

•

As the speedboat approached, none of them could believe how massive Blue Whales were. In comparison, sitting on the whale's head was a tiny lobster, jumping up and down, waving, as the crew skilfully positioned themselves next to the enormous whale.

"Finally, Clara, we meet, and this must be your mum. Enchanté, mademoiselle."

"I'm so happy to meet you," beamed Clara. "I, erm, didn't realise you were fish… I mean, not human," stuttered Clara, not really sure how to greet sea creatures politely. She tried again. "Um! Did you have a pleasant swim?"

Reuben and William's eyes widened.

"It was… interesting," replied William. "Perhaps you'd like to hear more."

"Yes, please! Is that OK, Mum?"

Amanda was still struggling to believe that she and her daughter were talking with a whale and a lobster.

"Erm… What about your party?" asked Amanda.

"Ahh, wee. You are 13 today. Happy birthday! William is 70 but I am younger. He still has all his teeth, though. All 350 of them. I've counted," Reuben said. "When he was asleep."

Everyone laughed, whilst the huge whale simply shook his head. It was clear that having Reuben as a friend could not be easy.

"Perhaps you should give Clara her phone back," William suggested.

"Oh, wee. Here eet ees, safe and sound. And chère, you would never have forgotten your sister. She would always be inside here."

Reuben placed his claw over his heart, before passing the phone to Clara.

"Thank you. I don't know how I can repay you both for your kindness," said Clara, her eyes glistening with tears.

Clara's mum placed an arm around her shoulder.

"No need, Clara," said William. "If we all try to look beyond what is important for ourselves and put others first, we will see the world in all its glory. We are not so different. We laugh, cry, share our lives and in time lose those we love. It is what binds us together on our journey to the stars."

"That is beautiful, William," sniffed Clara.

"And, if humans stopped dumping their rubbish in the sea, we would be a lot happier! And what he said," added Reuben, a huge grin on his face.

Everyone laughed, as Clara leant forward and embraced her two new friends — which was not as easy as it sounds. But between two arms, a flipper and a claw, they somehow managed it — and it was a moment they would never forget.

Whilst Amanda returned to get ready for the party, Clara spent the next two hours listening awestruck to the incredible story of the courageous whale and the brave lobster. She couldn't believe how much they were willing to sacrifice for someone they'd never met and wondered how they had survived.

As she listened, Clara realised what she wanted to do with the rest of her life. Their story would go onto inspire not only Clara, but, perhaps one day, her children and maybe even her grandchildren. Time passed quickly as the friends chatted and was sad when the officer told her it was time for him to return her safely to the Ocean Star. There was so much she still wanted to discover about Reuben and William's lives and the wonderful world in which they lived.

Clara smiled and watched as the magnificent Blue Whale and heroic lobster made their way majestically towards the harbour entrance. Today was a birthday she would never forget, and she couldn't wait to share their amazing story with her mum and in time the rest of the world.

•

Whilst Clara partied the night away with her mum, passengers and crew, William and Reuben could finally relax. It was a warm, clear night and the heavens were awash with stars. Their journey had been fraught with danger, yet somehow, they had made it through together.

The joy on Clara's face after being reunited with her phone was the only reward necessary. Rueben, meanwhile, had been thinking about all the gadgets humans used and whether they should become more modern sea creatures.

"Do you think we should get a mobile?" asked Reuben, as a shooting star sailed silently overhead.

"No!"

"What about a tablet?"

"No!"

"Sea-pods. Giant one's for you."

"I think it's past your bedtime."

"Do whales even have ears? I have never seen yours."

"About now Reuben," chuckled William, "I really wish I didn't!"

The End

Epilogue

Clara never forgot William and Reuben, who had risked their lives to return her mobile safely. On leaving school, their bravery inspired her to study marine biology, and she dedicated the rest of her life to protecting our world's precious oceans.

Clara also became one of the world's leading whale experts and she campaigned tirelessly to keep the oceans free from pollution. Because of her pioneering work, countless numbers of sea creatures and coral reefs thrived.

Years later, Clara also married Raphael, an underwater wildlife cameraman from France, and they had three, beautiful children of their own: *Stephanie, William,* and *Reuben*.

As for William and Reuben, well, let's just say their well-deserved holiday to Bermuda was a lot more eventful than they had planned. But that's another story…

Oh! Just in case you were wondering, Quickgill made it back safely to his wife - Suntide, and daughter Moonsong.

Index